Hemingway in Hawaii

Ray Pace

Copyright © 2017 by **Ray Pace**

Ray Pace
P.O. Box 384751
Waikoloa, HI 96738
raypacewrites@gmail.com

Publisher's Note: This is a work of fiction. Names, characters, places, and incidents are a product of the author's imagination. Locales and public names are sometimes used for atmospheric purposes. Any resemblance to actual people, living or dead, or to businesses, companies, events, institutions, or locales is completely coincidental.

Book Layout © 2014 BookDesignTemplates.com

Hemingway in Hawaii/ Ray Pace. -- 1st ed.
ISBN-13: 978-1547108848

This book is for Harry Wishard and the wonderful writers who make up the Hawaii Writers Guild. We rise together through story.

"Fiction is the lie through which we tell the truth."

Albert Camus

Hemingway in Hawaii

Foreword

Hemingway in Hawaii is about two brothers, Ernest and Leicester Hemingway, separated by 16 years. One was a literary god, the other a talented, highly competent writer subject to the ups and downs of a writer's career.

This book is in two sections.

The first section is "Hemingway's Hawaii Letter." It is a work best labeled historical fiction. Many of the characters in this work were real people. Leslie Wishard, Charles Clapp, Martha Gellhorn, and the Hemingways are some of them.

Others are figures of my invention, Colonel Demarest, Jack Wong, and Floyd Martin to name a few.

Though Corporal James Jones did exist in Hawaii during the time covered, there is no record of Jones ever having driven a staff car to deliver Ernest Hemingway to Schofield Barracks. There is plenty of evidence of James Jones's later literary abilities, *From Here to Eternity* and *The Thin Red Line* being the more well-known of his books.

Many of the incidents described in "Hemingway's Hawaii Letter" are based on fact. Ernest Hemingway was a spy for Treasury Secretary Henry Morgenthau, who suspected war with Japan was inevitable. Later conjecture that Ernest was also a spy for the Soviets has found currency among some and all out rejection by others who cite the incompetence and pettiness of FBI Director J. Edgar Hoover.

Ernest did fly from Oahu to the Big Island of Hawaii in February 1941 to determine the manner in which a possible trophy Black Marlin had been caught, and he did go up the slopes of Mauna Kea to shoot a Bighorn Sheep. The crash of the B-18 on the slopes of Kohala is not only well-documented, but part of the fuselage is still in a ditch on the mountain.

The second section of the book is called "Epilogue." All of it is true.

I thought that I was on to new horizons with the publication of *Hemingway, Memories of Les*. I had written a well-received book about my friend. It was time to move on to other literary pursuits.

Then, I walked into Harry Wishard's art gallery on the Big Island in early 2015. A walk through the place revealed a photo of Ernest Hemingway, rifle in hand, with a dead Bighorn Sheep. I asked Harry about it, and he explained what he knew of Hemingway's visit to the Big Island and how Harry's grandfather had been a part of the Hemingway trip up the mountain to shoot the Bighorn.

"One of the paniolos brought a bottle of his special booze," Harry said. "He told Ernest they'd drink it after they shot a trophy animal. They shot it, and they sat and drank the whiskey. It was just cheap rotgut."

Later visits to Harry Wishard brought more memories from relatives who knew at least a part of the story. How many times they went up the mountain to get the trophy varied, but the essence of the tale was still there. Hemingway came, he drank, he fished, and he shot. It sure sounded like Ernest Hemingway to me.

Photos started to round out the story and the times. Here were shots of B-18s, here was a shot of Martha Gellhorn with a rifle on horseback. There were stories on the Big Island and on Oahu that featured Hemingway and Gellhorn, but neither had written a word about any of it in any concise way. The story of Hemingway in Hawaii was told by others: a newspaper clip here, an oral account there. There were a few photos and a lot of memories, many rapidly fading about World War II, Hemingway, and Hawaii.

The Hemingway/Gellhorn stopover in Hawaii was just part of a larger trip to China where the two would attempt to find the truth about Chiang Kai Shek and Mao Tse Tung. Were their armies worth anything against the Japanese? What about the British in Hong Kong and Singapore? Would they be any help or would they fold?

The big story stateside, concerning Hemingway and Gellhorn, before the two left on their trip, was that Gary Cooper and Ingrid Bergman would star in the movie version of *For Whom the Bell Tolls*. Hemingway and Gellhorn had spent time with Cooper on his ranch before meeting with Bergman in San Francisco just before boarding the ship to Honolulu.

Whatever the Hawaii stopover had to offer wasn't worth much, according to the scribes of the day. Hawaii was a peaceful respite for the couple, a short honeymoon. The real war was in the Far East where Chinese nationalists had a shaky coalition with Mao's communists to battle the Japanese. That's where the big story was.

I had learned as a reporter that no matter what my colleagues in the media said, there was often more than one big story. Once while covering a large drug trial in Federal Court in Florida, I wandered down the hall to where a Coast Guard hearing was being held about a dive boat captain who in a panic during a storm had left his divers seven miles out at sea. While my colleagues from other news outlets were being bored by delays at the drug trial, I had wandered into a story of panic and malfeasance that no one else seemed to know about or maybe cared about. Their big story, after all, was down the hall.

My editors loved the story of the inept captain and the abandoned divers. The Miami News once again was showing what a poor newspaper its rival, the Miami Herald could be.

I would do it again covering the spread of AIDS in Key West.

Someone was deliberately infecting people with the disease. Rival news outlets assumed that taking handouts from the Monroe County Board of Health and attending county commission meetings devoted to HIV prevention posters was the big story.

I decided a bit of digging wouldn't hurt. Who was this latter day version of a Typhoid Mary? Why was this so out of control?

I developed a source in the Board of Health. Confidential information couldn't be released, but it could be strongly hinted at. It didn't take long using street sources to find out that the problem was the owner of one of the famous bars on Duval Street. He had an endless supply of new sex partners who were flattered by attentions from a man who ran one of the saloons where Ernest Hemingway. Jimmy Buffet and Tennessee Williams had once partied.

The story made a big splash. At least one pregnant woman sued the bar owner shortly before he died of HIV, and the story behind my story was written up in Fine Line, a journal that dealt with ethics in journalism. Digging had paid off with a big story.

Hawaii was to be different.

The more I kept digging on what the real story might have been in Hawaii, in February 1941, the more

I found holes. The piece couldn't be straight reporting.
Hemingway and Gellhorn had landed in Honolulu.
They had ridden horses up Mauna Kea to shoot a
Bighorn Sheep. If there was a story, it held truths better
expressed through fiction.

Hemingway and Gellhorn had left strong clues
while they were in Hawaii. It would be up to me to
patch together a story from those clues.

What follows is that effort.

Ray Pace, June 2017

Hemingway's Hawaii Letter

Part One

Miami, September 1982. Hot air clings wet to everything. Clouds build in the Everglades waiting to come roaring with thunder in a late afternoon assault on the beachfront. Somewhere in the Gulfstream below the Keys a low pressure forms, but on the isle of San Marino, tucked between mainland Miami and Miami Beach a faint breeze stirs off the Bay and is picked up inside the large house by the overhead fan above the dining room table.

He sits at the table sipping the glass of iced tea and swallowing the two pain pills that are supposed to numb his legs for a while. He opens the large folder that holds the letter from his brother from some forty years ago.

Feb 17, 1941

To: Les Hemingway

C/O PM Newsroom

Sixth Avenue and Bergen Street

Brooklyn, New York

Dear Baron,

I could tell you I'm writing this from the paradise of Hawaii, but that would be a goddamn lie. I'm sitting pretty, floating along at 180 miles an hour on this spacious airplane, a Pan American Clipper that has bunks for 36

people - a seaplane that they say will eventually get us to Hong Kong.

Miss Marty is anxious to see what all the fighting in China is about and I have enlisted as tour guide, caretaker, chauffeur and bartender for the duration.

Don't get me wrong; this is a Hawaii letter in which I will tell of the trials and tribulations involving this best-selling author and his wonderful missus. Yes, I know the book is doing well, although it's hard to get reports out here from Scribners. That whole crew is hard to contact over this large ocean. Must be all the saltwater jumbling things up.

I digress and will continue to digress in part so no one gets confused and tries to publish this as a dispatch to *PM*. Anyway, we had a time with Gary Cooper and crew in California. He'll be doing the movie version of Robert Jordan. Young Swede actress Ingrid Bergman will be co-starring. Saw her in San

Francisco before getting on the ship that delivered us to Honolulu. Very talented. Even her ear lobes are perfect. Could be a big star.

We were supposed to have flown to Hawaii, but things got changed and we climbed onto a ship instead. Five days after departing the Golden Gate Bridge, we arrived at Aloha Tower February 5.

I'm sure that one of the great truths of life will be that it's impossible to sneak into Honolulu on the *Matsonia*. Our plans for a quiet stay in the tropics got their great comeuppance before we even set foot on shore. Blasts of the ships horn were returned by a shouting crowd of maniacs who soon would be hugging us while attempting to strangle us with about 18 flowered leis, a sure-fire way of giving us a fair sampling of insects to crawl about our necks.

After that, the biggest affront was getting "Aloha-ed" by every one capable of

shouting it. The natives were way too friendly.
I kept looking for the hustle or the knife.
Chicago, New York, and Havana will do that
to you. I told Miss Marty that I felt like
spitting into the mouth of the next person who
said "Aloha."

But before I could there was salvation.
This big Hawaiian jumped out of the crowd
and yelled that he could drink Hemingway
under the table. Goddamn it, Les, I damn near
pissed in my pants laughing. We ended up
having our pictures taken together - the big
guy, Miss Marty and me.

But, damn. The big guy didn't bring
anything to drink with him and about that
time reporters muscled in to ask all sorts of
questions.

"How was *For Whom the Bell Tolls*
doing?"

"Was there a movie from the book?"

"Would we get into the war?"

"What were we going to do in China?"

I did my best to answer the questions without sounding like some know-it-all. The book was doing fine, the movie was going to be great, there was a chance we'd get into the war and we were going to China to report on the war between Japan and the Chinese. I finally told them I wasn't in the predictions business. I was a guy who wrote about what happened.

We finally got to our beachside cabana in Waikiki where we got a chance to toss down some drinks before the next onslaught - English Professors from the University of Hawaii. Yes, they have a university and even more so they have English professors that would happily bore the bejeezus out of damn near everyone with their references to trochee, allusion, and any eighteen syllable term designed to kill whatever life might be found in the simplest and most sincere expressions of humanity.

The stuffed shirts gathered in a place called the Willows Restaurant. Were there any willow trees around the islands? No one seemed to know. No one seemed to care. They did what they could to strangle the life out of my work while being ever so polite. All this happened without so much as a glass of beer in my hands. I finally spotted a couple bottles of Chianti someone had tied to a rafter for decoration. "Me thirsty," I said. "Hemingway need drink," I cave-manned at them. Finally one of the waiters got the message and served up several glasses.

I had been hoping for salvation from this group, but I should have kept my hopes under wraps. A car pulled up to take us to another luncheon, this one at dear old Aunt Grace's house. Yes, that one!

Miss Marty got it right when she said our luncheon companions were too boring to even be missionaries. We endured and finally got to our beach digs, but again to be followed around by reporters who wanted to see me walk on coral. Jeezus! I thought maybe I should just walk on top of the water and get it over with. Second Coming! Hemingway Turns Water into Wine!

We escaped again. After enduring more pablum speech at another function, we returned to the hotel, but this time found a savior of our own, a young reporter from the Star-Bulletin who brought a short story from a friend and a bottle of Scotch. I found both to be more than worthy and the young reporter, Martin was a good companion as we talked our way through Gertrude Stein, Dos Passos and the civil war in Spain. We could have covered several other civil wars, but it was time for another dangerous foray into a luau

**dinner at Lady Dawson Johnson's, an old
friend from Paris.**

He put down the letter and sipped the iced tea.
Paris. He remembered hooking up with Ernest as the
Allies marched into the city. The Germans are done, he
said, but they don't know it yet. Like wounded sharks,
they still have a lot of kill left in them. They're ready to
kill and they're ready to die. They just want to prolong
the ugliness.

He thought about the wounded sharks and
wondered if that's what he had become. Legs seemed
to be there only to hurt and the pills were there only to
lie about how bad things were.

He picked up the letter and was back four decades.

It was crowded, and the house was very expensive, but not very elegant according to Miss Marty. Somehow money tends to conflict with good taste. I mentioned that to one of the hangers-on, and he loudly announced that he took issue with me on that and said, "I'll take that up with you outside." He burst out the patio door toward the garden. I gulped my drink, not knowing if it would still be there when I got back from pummeling this guy and headed after him only to find that the only action in the garden was between a

Navy lieutenant and one of the women hula dancers. Our offended friend had disappeared into the night.

The following morning we took a tour of the naval base at Pearl Harbor and the airfield adjoining it- Hickam Field. The great poobahs wanted us to be impressed with all the ships and planes lined up in neat rows, "displaying America's might," as they put it. The fact that Japanese fishing boats were just off shore didn't seem to bother anyone. "We're not at war with them," one of our scrambled eggs wearers said. "We'll have plenty of notice before they ever get this far, if there is a war with them."

The whole thing looked like someone playing a pat hand with three aces, not even caring if the other guy has a full house.

We were impressed by the pilots and their crews flying B-18s out of Hickam. Their latest exercises included instrument only night flying over Hawaii Island, the one they call the Big Island. I offered to go with on one of their flights, but got turned down. The higher ups didn't want Hemingway mucking up their war games.

He put the letter down. He thought about that term: "war games." Sounded innocent enough. No one gets hurt. It's all a damn game.

The Falklands were still smoldering from the latest round of War Game. The old men who ran the games sent younger men and women into the war end of it.

He had seen that end of it in France, smelled it and thrown up.

A tear ran down his cheek.

"Goddamn it. I shouldn't be losing it like this," he said out loud. It was the damn medication, he thought. Or am I just old and useless?

Somehow, there was comfort in reading words from forty years ago. How many wars ago? He couldn't count.

A pain shot through his left leg. He twitched.

His hand shook as he picked up the letter.

We did fly over to the Big Island, but it wasn't with the B-18s. It was a fish that got things started.

A visitor from California, Charles Clapp landed what they thought might be a world record black marlin off the town of Kona on the west side of the island. They had it in an icehouse in Honolulu. Clapp got wind of my being an official in the International Game Fishing Association and wanted to know if what he caught might be a record.

I went to the icehouse and discovered much of the fish missing. It had been skinned out. It was bill, head, bones and tail. Part of the meat was in packages in freezers on the Big Island, but I could tell Clapp had tied into a large marlin. It measured 13 feet long. Would I go over to check on how he caught it? What kind of tackle, what kind of chair?

We flew over the following day. The Big Island is a spectacular place with mountains hitting over 13,000 feet high. Lava fields and spectacular reefs are evident as you fly in. If you took away the mountains, the town of Kona could almost pass for Key West. Fishing is king on the coast. As you go inland and upward, cattle and sugar take over.

We were met by Leslie Wishard, a fine gent who manages the Kawiki Sugar Company. He's a guy who knows his way around fishing and hunting. After catching our breath at the Kona Inn, we went out after marlin, boating a couple, but neither was anywhere near the monster that Clapp caught.

I found the boat Clapp had used to catch the marlin, and it didn't take long to see that a lot was wrong with the way he caught the fish if he was going for a record. The boat had a sliding chair that could be pushed back and forth by a helper or two. They did the work while all the guy with the rod did was reel in the slack. No fair fight in that. The fish needs to be honored with a battle, not processed like a cow in a stockyard.

Many things can go wrong in boating a large fish. I've seen men impaled by the bill of the marlin and I've seen sharks attack a prize fish and turn it into bloody chum before it could be boated. Off Bimini a few years back, the sea turned red as one of us fought the fish while another fired bullets at the pack of sharks bent on stripping the large fish to the bones.

You might even get to a point where the fish is winning the battle, pulling the boat and tiring out the man with the rod

when the sharks appear and do the great fish in. We catch these beautiful monsters never knowing what battles they have already fought. Unlike men, we don't see their scars until they are boated.

He placed the letter on the table and struggled to his feet. He grabbed the back of the chair and made it to the refrigerator for more iced tea.

Back at the table, he looked toward the bay and the dock that kept an open skiff and a larger sailboat. Next to the window was the portrait of his brother, the one that appeared on the cover of the book, the one that became a bestseller, the one that only he could write, My Brother, Ernest Hemingway. That triumph was twenty years in the past. Never to be reached again and now there was the talk of taking his legs -amputation. A man could show his scars and be honored for them but it didn't prevent the sharks - the doctors from trying to tear his flesh.

He looked at the open skiff. The pain would prevent him from walking to the dock. It was possible to take a boat like that across the stream to Bimini where marlin hung from the wooden yardarm near Brown's Resort. He'd done it, but he'd never do it again. The pain would never let him get into the boat again.

He read some more from the letter.

We had excellent weather for fishing with daytime temperatures in the low 80s and a light on-shore breeze that would switch to the Southwest as we got three miles offshore. Trade winds making 20 knots picked up some easy swells and gave us a ride while we waited for the marlin.

Spinner porpoises, sea turtles - *honu* the Hawaiian word for them - followed the boat for short bursts, but if you looked back at the island you'd see the snow-capped peaks of Mauna Kea and Mauna Loa, sleeping volcanoes. Mauna Kea is the home of a goddess, Poli'ahu who wraps herself in a white cape. Mauna

Loa is the home of her rival, Pele, the goddess of fire and lava. They stare at each other across miles of empty sky, each in her element.

I asked Wishard about Mauna Kea. Could we go up it? What would we see?

"Bighorn sheep," he said. "Trophy size sheep. Tough to shoot. We'd work our way up from Waimea, ranch country." He had the guns, the gear and a guide who could take us up the mountain to where the goddess lived. First we'd make our way out of Kona along the road connecting the coast with cattle country.

We stopped at Wishard's to pick up our rifles. He asked if I was familiar with the Springfield 03.

"Hell yes," I said. "I loved firing the one I had in Africa."

He handed me a box of .30-06 soft tip cartridges. We stepped out into a meadow that went up slope from the house. About a hundred yards out were some old fence posts with old metal signs rusting away.

"Check out your sights on the posts," he said. "See if you can zero in on what you see."

The rifle was well cared for and responded just like the one in Africa. I was ripping the signs apart in no time. It was a pleasure to watch the metal and wood fly apart. I couldn't wait for a bighorn sheep to get in my sights.

We got into Waimea by car. If I didn't know better, I would have said we were in Idaho or Wyoming. Green mountains and hillsides covered with horses, cows, and sheep.

We stopped at one of the ranch houses where Wishard introduced us to the family. Nice place, well taken care of, but it seemed that their most prized possession was a pane of glass in their door where someone had taken a diamond ring and scratched "Boy Blue" into it. I didn't connect until Wishard said that Boy Blue was King Kalakaua who would come over to the Big Island to race his prize horses and to drink whiskey.

Miss Marty asked if the old boy was still around and that brought a few grins from the family. What was so funny?

Wishard said the old king was long dead, but there might be some of the old boy left behind.

"Some nights they hear rumbling in some of the rooms where the king used to stay. They go check and nothing there. They close a window in the room and in the morning it's back open. Haven't found any empty booze bottles, yet."

It got me thinking where I might hang out after I crap out. I could take over a bar stool at the Floridita in Havana or sit in Sloppy Joe's in Key West and bug the piss out of Joe Russell. I wouldn't opt for Harry's New York Bar in Paris right now - too many Nazis. One Nazi is too many.

He leaned back in his chair and propped the right leg up on the footstool. It felt better. He thought Ernest wouldn't be at the Floridita, unless he thought his ghost could raise havoc among the bureaucratic communists who were hanging out there these days. As far as Sloppy Joe's, Key West was full of Ernest look-alikes. For all he knew Ernest WAS down there, pretending to be a phony Ernest Hemingway.

He smiled. The thought of Ernest's ghost hanging out in a bar had him. Another thought had him smiling too. Harry's New York Bar in Paris.

He was with Ernest when they "liberated" Harry's from the Nazis in the summer of forty-four. There weren't any Nazis on site, but Ernest said it was because they turned tails and ran like the rats they were. "They aren't up for a good fight and they don't deserve a good bar." "Liberating" Harry's was one of Ernest's favorite activities. He had done it several times with a wide assortment of "liberators." Ernest was also fond of "liberating" the bar at the Ritz Hotel where the

Luftwaffe had been headquartered during the Nazi Occupation.

When Les became a ghost where would he hang out?

Maybe one could travel around, check in with friends and relatives to see how they were doing? You probably couldn't talk directly with them, but maybe you could call them up at night to hear their voice when they'd answer, or maybe you could appear to someone your friend knew and ask about him. They'd tell you a bit of news and later they'd tell your friend, "A guy was in here the other day, asking about you. Gave him your number, damn if he didn't look like Les Hemingway."

He smiled and went back to the letter.

Just down the road from the haunted ranch house we met our guide who would take us to the bighorns. Our horses were ready along with a couple of pack mules.

"This is Santiago," Wishard said. "He's one of the best paniolos around and he knows the mountain like sharks know the smell of blood."

Paniolo is what people in Hawaii call a cowboy, Les.

I looked at Santiago. He was leathery and God knows how old. His skin looked like a dried-out cigar, but his handshake was one of iron.

"You Ernesto?" he asked. "I gonna take you up the mountain and you gonna shoot a bighorn weigh 400 pound and then we gonna sit and get drunk. I brought a special bottle to celebrate."

I asked him where he was from.

"Before this, Los Gatos, south of San Francisco. I take people there to the mountain to kill the lions. They used to wander into town. I worked a ranch there. Lions would attack the cows. I told them I could track the lions, but if they were going to shoot they needed better rifles, not some shotgun for birds. You gotta get close with a shotgun. The lion would have to eat the barrels while you pulled the triggers. I took them to an outfitter in San Francisco. They were happy, took me to the Seals game. Got to see DiMaggio before he was a Yankee. I'd listen to their games on the radio."

Wishard slapped Santiago on the back and said, "Let's go. We'll talk later after we give our guest a chance at a trophy."

We rode for several hours, climbing toward the white-capped peak of Mauna Kea. It got colder. Wishard broke out some heavy parkas that looked like leftovers from the Russian front in the Great War. We were happy to have them. The sun sank into the ocean and we were soon bundled up in tents near the small fire.

"In the morning, you shoot your Bighorn," Santiago said.

"How high are we?" I asked.

"Maybe nine thousand feet," Wishard said. "Santiago knows where they'll be in the morning. It's a short walk, maybe a mile up that draw. You'll go with him and get your shot. The rest of us will stay here."

The short walk turned into a half-day trudge through busted lava and scrub plants. Then in the early afternoon, we saw it standing majestically on a rocky ledge. Santiago turned and smiled.

I hesitated for a moment. A shot to the heart would bring the animal down in an instant, but something was telling me to shoot it in the head. It would be a difficult shot, but I knew I could do it. The rifle and I were one.

I aimed and fired.

The shot to the head was true and the animal crumpled to the ground.

"Ernesto," Santiago yelled. "What
I tell you? You got him!"

The Bighorn was 385 pounds. We drank
from Santiago's whiskey. The beast was
a magnificent kill.

Marty Gellhorn Hemingway on
Horseback

We never got to the top of Mauna Kea, but it was cold enough. We could feel the icy breath of the mountain as the wind came off the snow above us. The ancient Hawaiians made it all the way up without horses. Gutsy bastards, I'll give them that. I bet they didn't run around aloha-ing everyone every ten seconds.

We landed back in Honolulu on February 12 and to our delights, we were pretty much ignored by the newspapers and entourage of shirt-tail relatives and academic hangers-on. We got to our hotel where we ordered dinner and enjoyed some rum as we watched the sunset over the Pacific. Was this finally the belated honeymoon Miss Marty had promised us?

A letter from Scribners attested to 491,000 copies of *For Whom the Bell Tolls* being sold, but a telegram from the same source attested to only 425,000 copies. There they were on the table. Who was wrong, the typist in New York or the telegrapher from Western Union?

Another telegram from our friend at the Treasury Department asked me to meet with a Colonel Demarest while in Honolulu. Nothing else was said.

The next morning our phone rang while we were eating breakfast. Demarest would send a staff car for us and take us to Schofield Barracks near the town of Wahiawa. I would meet with Demarest. Miss Marty would get a tour of the latest in live-fire gunnery exercises. About an hour later we were on our way.

The friend at Treasury was Treasury Secretary Henry Morgenthau, Les knew. Ernest had met with a Morgenthau top aide. Could Ernest find out if we were prepared for the Japanese? Would Chiang Kai-Shek hold it together in China? What about the Communists under Mao? Was he a factor, or just a Russian puppet?

Though the United States was officially neutral, Morgenthau was working hard to find funding to fight Germany and Japan. Who could be a reliable partner?

How could any one man find all that out? Those were exciting days, but no one could foresee what was about to blow up in the face of America. If they could, who would listen?

Colonel Demarest had his clerk bring in coffee. Once the aide left, the colonel reached into his desk drawer and brought out a bottle of brandy. He poured us each a healthy shot into our cups.

"I could sit here listening to what you think, Hem, and I will, but goddamn it, I go first," he said. "You notice the bullshit we're drowning in out here? All the goddamn planes lined up wingtip to wingtip at Hickam? Battleship Row at

Pearl? That's what they call it. Sitting ducks in a shooting gallery."

He took a long pull on his cup and continued.

"The muckety mucks in Washington are behind this mess. They're getting rid of Admiral Richardson and replacing him with Admiral Kimmel. Richardson wanted the fleet to stay in San Diego where it could be supported and protected. That didn't go over, so Kimmel's in and Richardson is out."

"You're army," I said. "How does that get to you?"

"Damn good question, Hem. We're in charge of protecting the fleet while it's in port. We can send out our flyboys to check on who's getting close. You probably heard about the night flights of the B-18s over Hawaii Island. It's

instrument flying for the pilots, but
something extra for our boys on the
ground. We try to pick them up on a
radio beam sweep as they come back in.
Sometimes we see them, but a lot of times
we don't. The Brits have been working
on this. Call it radar. Could be a big help
if there was a large air attack, and if we
could get it to work."

"What about the local population. These
Hawaiians up for a fight if it comes?"

"Ain't just Hawaiians, Hem." He
poured more brandy into our cups. "We
got a mix of people here, Chinese,
Japanese, Filipinos, a few Koreans and
some of us white folks, haoles they call
us."

"So what happens if Japan gets us into
the war?"

"Good question. Could be a few doing sabotage, but most of the younger ones are baseball and hot dogs. They listen to big band music, Bing Crosby and read your books. Thing about the Japanese here - Many of them feel betrayed by Japan. The Japanese Americans are treated like they're lower class by the Japanese nationals. The real fanatics say the Japanese living here are traitors to the Emperor."

"Hell of a world," I said. "You got Hirohito in one ocean and Hitler in another."

"You left out Mussolini," he said.

"Yeah, every circus needs a clown." I said.

He looked me in the eye.

"I know you're looking for things out here for our friend at Treasury. I met him several times when I was stationed in D.C. I can feel this thing over here starting to explode. Could be an attack on the Philippines or, hell, maybe even here, but it's coming. It'll be terrible if war breaks out here. These islands are beautiful. A lot of service people think that Hawaii's just another port with whorehouses down on Hotel Street. No denying that, but you've seen Waikiki, you've seen the Big Island. A man could get lost out here and never care about going stateside."

What was my view on the situation? He leaned forward.

I told him I'd seen the same shooting gallery situation that he saw at Pearl and at Hickam.

"We're headed to China to see if the Generalissimo is all he's cracked up to be," I said. "I expect the Brits are getting

nervous with the Japanese getting closer
to Hong Kong. I'll be pouring some
brandy for them, picking their brains.
Our friend at Treasury has some
concerns over both the Limeys and
General Chiang."

He smiled and nodded.

"It's nice to know that I'm not alone in
this," he said. "If no one listens, it's going
to be shit."

"It's going to be shit even if they do
listen," I said.

I picked up Miss Marty outside
Demarest's office. She was waiting in the
staff car that would take us back to
Waikiki.

"They took me into the Waianae
Mountains and showed me gun
emplacements," she said. "From up there

you can see far out to sea. That could be where an attack might come from."

"Think they could repel an attack?" I asked.

"I kept feeling I had been in this situation before," she said.

"Where?" I asked.

"In Spain, just before the Loyalists fell apart."

He got up and hobbled to the door. Sore legs or not, he didn't want to fall apart. He opened the door and stepped out. The sun felt warm on his bare legs. He looked down and saw how spindly they had become. Diabetes did that. He saw the scars where the doctors had made their first pass.

The boats bobbed as the wake of a large sloop passed the dock. The guy at the wheel waved. Headed to Bimini? Headed to the Keys? Hell, could be Hawaii.

He stumbled his way back into the house and sat down at the table. He looked at the letter. Things were different then. He had been working in New York, freezing his way through February and reporting for PM, what some referred to as a great experiment in newspapers. Erudite, sophisticated, destined to lose money and eventually go down the drain, but a great place to connect. Good bars, lots of characters. Reporters from all the dailies would gather and drink.

Everyone had a theory. The Japs would never attack. Britain was done for. We'd end up with Canada. China would beat back the Japanese. The communists would fall apart in China. They were all wrong.

Better to talk about the Yankees and their chances, or what was on Broadway. At least nobody got killed if you were wrong.

He remembered the good-natured kidding.

"Les, let me buy you a beer. When your book takes off like your brother's, I want to be able to tell them I knew you back when."

"Hemingway, for whom the bar bill tolls."

"You go visit him down in Cuba? Never mind him. Tell us about those crazy Cuban babes."

There were the crazy Cuban babes and some 20 years later there would be the book, My Brother, Ernest Hemingway. There would be the interviews, the Playboy magazine articles about him and his brother. They wouldn't be using that phrase like they did when his novel got mixed reviews: "The importance of being Ernest." No, they'd give him respect because the book sold well and if nothing else, the critics understood money. Only a handful referred to "the importance of being Ernest's brother."

To hell with them. Sycophants and toadies. Without their theories and their attitudes they were small and bitter men who couldn't imagine an adventurous life of their own so they had to invent one for his brother. Hemingway who could do everything, drink a gallon of whiskey, hunt big game, land big fish, write bestsellers, all in the same day! They made you want to go around with dirty hands and face and chew tobacco and spit on their Italian loafers.

He laughed at the thought of spitting on them and sat back at the table to read more.

Floyd Martin, the reporter who brought the short story and the scotch met us at our cabana. You had to get out among the people, he said. There's a pretty decent bunch that lives here.

He had a Jalopy the three of us could fit into. We drove out past Diamond Head to a fish shack restaurant that looked as if it might fall into the bay.

"Don't worry," he said. "It's been falling into the bay for years. Hope you weren't expecting one of those streamlined art-deco diners."

Miss Marty said she hated the art deco attempts at civility. I told him it was fine, even if it did fall into the bay.

It was some of the finest seafood I've had. It was served on a platter with avocado, mango and papaya in abundance.

"They're not doing this because they think we're special?" I asked.

"They must think everyone's special," Martin said. "Look around."

The place was packed with people of all sizes and shades and each table had platters just like ours. Pitchers of beer or carafes of wine were on each table. You wouldn't call it great wine, but it was good and for what we ate, the price was reasonable.

Martin introduced us to the owner, a Chinese American named Jack Wong. He came out of the kitchen wearing an apron that had seen plenty of use. His wife came with him and introduced herself as Nora.

"Nora Taniguchi," she said. "But now my name is Wong. More better to be Chinese these days, so I let Jack Wong think he's in charge." She smiled.

Jack Wong sat down on the bench next to me. He offered his hand after wiping it on his apron.

"Jeezus, I read all your books. No bullshit. I majored in English Lit at University of Hawaii, but that didn't destroy me. I could have been a teacher, but I'd rather catch fish and run this crazy restaurant. Think I'm nuts?"

"Only in the best of ways," I said.

"I hear you're headed to China?"

"Your old home?" I asked.

"Never been there," he said. "My dad came over as a young kid, worked the sugar cane, got into working a store in Chinatown, ended up owning it.

You'd like him, Tough as nails on the outside, heart of gold hiding inside."

"What's your dad think about the war over there?" I asked.

"He says it was Hell when he left and it's still Hell. War or no war, the little guy gets screwed."

After dinner, Martin drove us out past Makapu'u point toward a town called Waimanalo. There were lots of horses and a hilly beach where we stopped.

"Legend says that sometimes Madam Pele the volcano goddess hangs out on this road," Martin said. "She appears as either a good looking wahine or an old bag. If you stop and give her a ride your luck will change, sometimes for the better, sometimes for the worse."

Miss Marty laughed.

"Is the beautiful young wahine the one that brings trouble?" she asked.

"Don't they always?" I said.

Martin said Hawaiian culture was full of contradictions. Sharks were not only a menace to many but to some families they were considered guardians - aumakua- sort of a god that watched out for the family. He told of one legend where an old woman thinking her days were over went down to the ocean and walked in so she could be taken by sharks. A shark did grab her, but it tossed her back on the shore, telling her that it wasn't her time. She must take care of her grandson. The grandson went on to become a doctor and the old woman lived another twenty years.

I thought about the shark as both the savior and the destroyer, the protector and the threat. It was true that they were vicious beasts that were only too happy to kill, but they were also survivors capable of living on damn near any diet. I told Martin about gutting sharks and finding license plates inside their stomachs. Pieces of pelican, pieces of someone's family dog, along with beer bottles and fishing lures- all could be found in their gut.

Martin said he had heard similar tales about politicians. I added book critics and radio preachers to the mix. Miss Marty jumped in with maître des at over-priced restaurants and hairdressers who referred to themselves as "Mister" so and so.

Well, Les we never did figure out all this theology about the shark, but it was an interesting exercise in seeing if a villain could be redeemed.

Martin brought up one thought that would be hard to prove either way.

"Out of all the people taken by sharks, how many do you think really had it coming?" Martin asked. "Think about it. You don't think they were all innocent babes, do you?"

I had to admit he had me. He didn't have Miss Marty, though. She started making a list of people who the shark could dine on.

He smiled. Ernest was at his best when you got him going in a meaty conversation or when he would enlist everyone around the table to contribute to a story. He'd start it off with part of the first sentence.

"I had a lot to drink one night in a seedy bar in Havana so I walked outside for a breath of fresh air and I saw..."

It would be the person to his left who would pick up the tale:

"...a donkey painted pink and pulling a cart with three orange..."

Handed off to the next person on the left:

"...mandolin players and a very large..."

"...tuba player who was actually a member of Parliament who had run away from..."

"...his wife because she had threatened to..."

"...tell the king that Spanish spies were hiding in his..."

The game would go on around the table. The story would have people laughing and spitting their drinks and then someone would break it off and go into their own outrageous tale about a king who had Spanish spies hiding in his wine cellar or maybe a tale of painted donkeys and orange tuba players they had seen at Mardi Gras.

It was priming the pump, Ernest said. It made you think about story. What you could get away with and what would never fit in. Life presented the same absurdities, he'd say. You just had to pick and choose. The story was out there; you just had to cut away all the stuff that wasn't the story.

Had he taken Santiago off Mauna Kea and put him into a leaky boat off Havana? Had Clapp's fish been cleaned with a knife in Kona or been victimized by sharks in the Gulf Stream?

There were those who said that Ernest was at his peak as a writer when he had finished For Whom the Bell Tolls. Was he putting together what became The Old Man and the Sea at the same time? Was that where the creation was and the following years were years of editing a small masterpiece and putting out lesser works the critics and the public merely accepted?

The critics and the public were fickle. Some family members could be worse, he thought. Ernest's son Gregory had begged for help from his uncle Les. The book was Papa. Though he didn't trust Gigi, as Gregory was known, he gave his all to the work, expecting some credit and some of the proceeds. It ended up in a court battle.

Where were all those honest critics then, he wondered?

Maybe they were busy attacking a prize marlin.

He read on.

When we got back to the hotel there was a message from Colonel Demarest: "Could we meet again in the morning? I'll have a staff car arrive at nine. Important."

Miss Marty decided she needed some rest and planned to visit the pool and do some reading. It was up to me to find out what Demarest wanted.

The staff car arrived. I sat up front with the driver, a young corporal, James Jones. I told him I hadn't eaten.

Could we stop and I'd buy him breakfast?

He pulled into a diner. I wanted to get the view from an enlisted man. We sat in one of those over-stuffed booths and ordered up some ham and eggs with coffee.

The kid turned out to be from Illinois and had read a couple of my books. He said he was interested in writing about some of the experiences he had in the army.

"Like what?" I asked.

"Writer to Writer, sir?" He asked.

"Yeah, I said. "I'll only steal the good parts and never tell any of your cohorts where I got it. And knock off the 'sir' part. Call me 'Ernest' or 'Hem' or 'Hey You'. I'm just another guy who likes to catch fish and watch boxing matches."

He laughed.

"What's so funny?" I asked.

"I'm on the boxing squad," he said. "Someone tell you about that?"

I was laughing, too.

"Hell no," I said. "Coincidence?"

"Only if you believe in them, Sir, I mean Hem."

Jones warmed up after that exchange.

"There's a lot of the hurry up and wait going on over here," he began. "I hear a lot of talk about war, and what will happen if we're attacked. Hard to say from a corporal's view."

"What about a writer's view?" I asked.

"A lot of young kids here that can't find their dicks and a lot of old men putting in their time until retirement. Even over in Manila there's an old man in charge, MacArthur. Word is he's waiting for the old soldier's home to grab him."

"Demarest seems like a sharp guy?"

"Yeah, I hear that's why they're shipping him out. The army doesn't like it when you rock the boat. Personally, I like him. Maybe that means they'll be shipping me out, too."

"But you're on the boxing squad?"

"Yeah, I do okay at that, so I guess they might keep me here for awhile. There's lots of competition between units on that. Lots of money exchanges hands. They say it's good for morale. I can't say I can see any big boost. Like I say, kids and guys waiting to retire."

We drove past cane fields up the valley toward Schofield. You would swear it was a summer day somewhere in the Carolinas, but we were in winter in the middle of the Pacific and maybe on the verge of getting into a war holding three aces to someone else's full house.

Demarest greeted me at his office door and motioned for me to sit down in front of his desk. No coffee or brandy this time. I looked around and things looked empty.

"I'm packed and ready for shipping out," he said. "I'll be joining Mac Arthur in the Philippines."

I asked how he felt about that.

"I hear that it's worse over there than it is here, but I'll do what I can with what they give me, Hem. The guy I'm replacing is retiring back to Oregon, and a couple of the officers on his staff are headed back that way at the end of this year. Doesn't sound like dashing heroes in that bunch."

Did our friend at Treasury have anything to do with this?

"I'll find a way to get reports to him, but this is starting to look like a done deal. The Japanese just get more aggressive and the rest of the world just looks on hoping they'll go away. Well guess what? They ain't going away."

Did he think we were up to taking on the Japanese?

"Yeah, if we're looking to get a good ass whupping.

I could show you requisition forms that are backlogged from here to Detroit. We get recruits in here that are one step away from going to prison or going to a TB sanitarium. We're still using rifles from the Spanish War and I wouldn't be surprised if they shipped us muskets and long rifles that General Washington requested back in 1781."

He said he'd be gone the next day. I asked him if I could buy him a drink somewhere. We got back into the staff car and drove into Wahiawa.

It was a military town. Bars, tattoo parlors, and whore houses. The nameless joint we went into had some class. It backed up onto a small lake with an outdoor patio. Demarest brought Corporal Jones into the place with us.

"You don't mind, Hem, do you?" He asked.

"Hell no, I like James just fine," I said. "We're both writers."

A large pitcher of beer arrived.

"For today, let's say 'Fuck the War'," Demarest said. "Tell us about catching the big fish in the Gulfstream. Tell us about the women in Cuba."

There were big fish in the Gulfstream and soon after the war broke out Ernest would be going after them - German submarines. Pilar became a boat loaded with exotic weapons, bazookas, machine guns, hand grenades. Miss Marty had tried to do a story on the bumbling Nazis in Cuba, but when she began to realize that they weren't so bumbling her editors lost interest. Collier's Magazine was a fine example, he thought, of the experts in New York or Washington deciding on the script while the actors found it to be different and dangerous to stick to their lines.

Finally someone got the idea that the U-boats were really sinking part of the merchant fleet. What could be done? Who did we have down there? Enter Hemingway.

He smiled.

They never caught a sub, but got plenty of toys to play with. Pilar always had a full tank and extra jerry cans full of fuel. In fact, she was a floating bomb. It was a wonder that none of the rolled-in-Havana cigars everyone smoked hadn't blown everyone to kingdom come. Maybe with all the rum came immunity - drunks and children lead charmed lives.

Miss Marty said Ernest was crazy. One night in the Floridita, he sat guessing at how soon he'd catch a Nazi sub and blow it out of the water with the innocent looking Pilar that seemed equipped for catching much smaller fish than the German brand.

"You'll all get killed," she said. "Then I'll have to sit in this joint all alone drinking their damn daiquiris and listening to people telling me you were all nuts - something I gladly attest to."

**Floyd Martin had another man
he wanted us to meet, a kahuna,
someone who was in touch with the old**

religion, what the Hawaiians believed in before the Christian Missionaries arrived with their New England ways and dress. We drove up into Palolo Valley. The road eventually became two ruts that led us over several wooden bridges with mountain streams under them. Jungle covered our pathway and colorful birds darted in front of us.

We expected someone dressed in beads and woven grass, I guess. Instead, we pulled up to a well-designed cabin with a Hawaiian in slacks and polo shirt sitting at a table, drinking beer from a bottle.

"This is Kimo," Martin said.

Kimo got up and shook our hands and motioned for us to sit down at the table. He produced three bottles of beer from an ice-chest.

He was quick to get to the point. He wasn't going to be a guy offering mumbo jumbo. He had an ax to grind, and he jumped right to it.

"Hemingway, I read your book about the Spanish Civil War. I felt the passion of the people, the downtrodden in their battle against fascists. My people have the same problems here, except we have really no means to fight back. We've been taken over by a strange religion and a foreign power. We are a colony of your country and we're getting the short end of the stick."

I said that I thought a kahuna was concerned with spiritual problems, not with politics.

"Tell me where your spirit ends," he said. "Does your body know freedom that your soul can only hope for?"

"Good question," I said. "You sit here up in the hills pondering these things while the world below goes on its way to what? War?"

"Yes, war," he said. "This war will change the world. Many will die and borders will change. Americans somehow think they are immune. The destruction will begin soon."

"Japan?"

"Of course. They won't find any helpers here. They'll eventually lose, but you Americans will over-extend. You will lose, also. Look at the British. They may make it through the war, but they'll lose when peace comes. They can't afford their colonies. They can't even pay their way in the war. America is propping them up. You'll see when you get to Hong Kong. The Brits are hanging on by a thread."

I thought about what he said. I asked him how Hawaii would come out of the war he was sure we were headed for.

"Hawaii will always be the prize colony of America," he said. "The day may come when they call us a state, but we have little in common with the states in your union. The kama'aina, the whites who have lived here a long time understand this. They try to go back to America and find that they no longer fit in. Something has happened to them out here, and there's no going back."

I thanked him for his hospitality as we got back into Martin's car. He shook my hand and held it in a firm grip as he looked me in the eyes.

"Write the book, Ernest," he said. "The one about struggle. The one

**you have been thinking about. It will be
your best."**

**We had been talking about war
and how borders would change and
countries would lose, but the only image
that came to mind as he said those
words was what was left of Clapp's
marlin, hanging in the icehouse. Bill,
head, bones and tail.**

He reached for the pill bottle. His legs were
hurting again. He sipped the iced tea and swallowed,
hoping for the numbness to come soon.

All those experts, he thought, this is what they
loved to argue about. They would write book after
book about how Ernest came up with the book that
won the Pulitzer and which led to his receiving the
Nobel Prize. Most of them had no talent for putting

together a story that could exist on several levels and be interesting even when read for the third time. They were bean counters. They didn't know, or care to know that sometime the muse hounded you for years, whispering in your ear as you were falling asleep or leaving a dream image in your mind as you awoke. You couldn't count the times you tried to remember those thoughts and images and were left with an empty feeling thinking about two words that didn't have any meaning, but still stuck in your head like some song that wouldn't go away.

He stood up and hobbled his way to the refrigerator for more iced tea. He looked at his battered legs. This would not go on long, he thought. He would decide. He would act, just as his father had, just as his brother had. Whatever lay beyond was either a wonderful adventure or a sudden exit into nothing.

He sat and read again.

As we rode down the mountain toward Waikiki, Martin explained that people like Kimo understood both the strengths and the limitations of encouraging Hawaiians to honor their heritage.

"They can only go so far," he said. "Many Hawaiians are part something else, Japanese, Chinese, Irish, Spanish, Portuguese. It's hard to fight the bloodline of the oppressor when the oppressor's blood is running through your veins."

No, the solution, Martin said was to honor the history and the heritage.

This was something that someone of
any ethnic background could
participate in. The Hawaiians of old
were great navigators. Anyone who
appreciated sailing could honor that.
The Hawaiians respected nature. There
were old ideas of spirituality that still
worked, he said. The old religion wasn't
all servitude, violence, and ignorance.
There was poetry in the old legends and
lessons that anyone could partake of.

I thought of the Hawaiian
navigators. Without compass, they
found their way by the stars, the
currents, the birds and the wind
patterns. They knew the seasons and
what each had in store for the sailor.
They were at home on the sea. They
didn't need the *Matsonia* to drag them
into Honolulu and they didn't worry
about making a crossing in record time

or facing the boss because they were delayed.

I thought also about how they put a face on snow and another face on lava, called them goddesses and created stories about their bitchiness. The ancient Greeks had this going for themselves. The Roman Republic could only steal the stories from the Greeks and put new names on the players.

The Hawaiians could create stories that held up to the passage of years. For that you had to honor them.

He sipped his iced tea. Ernest had created stories that would stand the test of time. There would always be a new interpretation of his work, another discovery of some bit of his work, a letter or two perhaps. It would have the critics talking and studying the new finding. There were still pieces of manuscript in Havana somewhere, or so it was rumored. Ernest was an industry. Whether you wanted it that way or not, fact was fact and even though there were facts, there would always be legend. Nobody could do everything that Ernest was said to have done, because Ernest hadn't done all of it himself.

Hemingway's Hawaii Letter

Part Two

Goddamn it Baron,

Here I am like some damn fool thinking I must have mailed this letter to you already and I'll be damned if I still have it in my bag. I'm not on my way to China anymore. I'm on my way back. I'm sitting here back in Honolulu waiting for a flight out to the States. It's May already, and I have to tell you that things don't look any better than they did before I flew out of here in February.

I met up with Colonel Demarest again. He joined me on our flight's last leg into Honolulu. Miss Marty was delayed down in Singapore where she went to see if

the Brits were handling things any better than they were in Hong Kong. Demarest was on Midway where he had stopped for a couple days. Anything important? I asked.

"Nuts and bolts stuff," was the reply.

Later as we buzzed our way toward Honolulu, we sipped from my flask and he opened up a bit more. The Old Man in Manila was losing it, Demarest said. He had looked over what the army had to work with and what they had to defend, and it looked pretty thin, as he put it.

I told him how the Brits were stretched thin in Hong Kong and were probably relying more on their hopes against the Japanese than anything that resembled military might.

Why was he headed back to Honolulu? He said he would see Admiral Kimmel and tell him what he thought about the situation in Manila. I told him I had been through there several days back and didn't see much value in the place at all. It was full of rude people who would come and knock on your hotel room door at all hours to ask stupid questions. I told Demarest that I almost regretted having a best seller out where anyone could read it and recognize me. I said I'd be happy to head for Havana where they'd have to wait for the translation to get there before they could bug me about it. By that time I'd be hiding up in the hills.

He remembered the Finca and how it sat above the city and how now the Cubans had taken Pilar and sat her next to the house where she was falling apart from dry rot. They wouldn't let her sit at the port or be dry-docked near the sea. It was Fidel. He wanted his Hemingway collection in the hills, all together where it could be watched and toured by the select who could make kind gestures to Fidel and Hemingway in the same breath or sentence- a sneaky way to tie a dictator to a famous writer who hated dictators.

The house in Key West was its rival. It was available to the masses. The six-toed cats still hung around. How many generations of cats could there be? You could drive to Key West in four hours or fly the hundred and twenty miles in no time at all. In the old days you could be in Havana in the same amount of time, but no more.

He couldn't drive anywhere anymore and flying would be difficult. The legs weren't working. You could only travel well in your mind and only if the pain pills were working.

Why was this letter from so long ago grabbing his attention and not letting go?

Was it because Ernest was at his peak and it was before the war changed everything and the country was still holding onto its innocence?

Or was it the impending doom that attracted him to this letter? The attack on Pearl Harbor? The Holocaust? The Bomb?

The happiness would fade. Ernest would have head injuries. Miss Marty would leave. Miss Mary would follow.

And then there was the gun. The double barrel shotgun with bird shot. Both barrels to the forehead. The paniolo, Santiago had said it, "... some shotgun for birds. You gotta get close with a shotgun. The lion would have to eat the barrels while you pulled the triggers." Or take the top of his head off where all those strange thoughts were coming from.

There were other guns, he thought. He went back to the letter.

When we got to Honolulu, Demarest had a staff car drop me back at the hotel in Waikiki. He said he'd call me and hoped we could get together for some drinks after he saw Kimmel. I phoned the newspaper and asked for Martin.

"Who's calling?" the woman wanted to know.

"Hemingstein," I said.

"Beg pardon?"

"Hemingstrudel."

"Thank you. Floyd, there's a Mister Strudelstein on the phone for you."

I damn near pissed in my pants laughing. I was surprised by my reaction. Maybe it was because I was back on American soil where people played jokes over the phone. I couldn't see the Chinese doing that. Chiang or Mao would take someone out and have them shot for that. That's who we were relying on over there to carry the ball, a couple of humorless guys who would get their army to solve all their problems with phone pranksters.

Martin came to the phone and started laughing the minute he heard my voice.

"Is your next novel going to be about China?" He asked without even saying hello.

"Yeah, I learned to say 'ma' with different inflections. Now I know whether I'm insulting someone's horse or their mother."

We met for drinks at the Royal Hawaiian in Waikiki. The veranda there had a view of the ocean and the barman was generous with the rum.

Martin wanted to know everything about the China trip and I wanted all the scuttlebutt about Hawaii's preparation for possible war. What had he heard?

"The B-18 flights are still going on over the Big Island," he said. "There was a bit of a setback, actually the day after you left for China. One of the planes lost an engine coming back from Hilo and

ended up bellying into a forest on Kohala-
the dormant volcano on the north end of
the island."

"How bad?" I asked.

"They all made it, some with light
injuries, but the plane is still up there,"
He said. "It fell off the trees and later
wound up in the gulch. They're saying
that the pilot did some fancy flying to
bring it in like that, especially at night.
It's all part of the new radar thing they're
trying to figure out."

I told him I was surprised that he
knew about the radar.

"Everyone knows about it," he said.
"Admiral Kimmel's staff has loose lips.
You'd be surprised what you can get out
of them for the price of a drink or two."

I told him that the Brits in Hong Kong
were just as bad. They must be counting

on something I didn't see. What I did see was a thinly manned defense line that wouldn't last long in the face of a Japanese attack.

"That's a hell of a story," he said. "You'll get a lot of readers interested in that one."

I told him it probably wasn't going to work that way. There were stories you told the public and then there were stories that you told to those who might be able to make a difference. I would be trying to make contact with those people when I got back to the States.

He nodded.

"I hope you can use whatever I've given you," he said. "The paper I work for isn't one that sticks its neck out. Garden party journalism, I call it. I learn a lot from the various drunks, but I can't get much of it into print."

I told him I wondered who else was listening to the drunks at the garden parties. How much of it was in the pipeline to Tokyo?

"That's a hard one to prove," he said. "I have my doubts about some of them, but no real proof. You go to a cocktail party and everyone serving the drinks and the food are Japanese. You get the impression they aren't too up on English, but then you wonder why the guy with the tray of pupus is standing there so long after everyone's taken from the tray."

We closed the bar and said our good nights. I told him I'd try to see him again before I shipped out. I got into bed wondering where Miss Marty was. Was she on her way back through Hong

Kong? I had some of her notes for her stories and I missed her sassiness. I went to bed thinking about the blue waters of the Gulfstream and how on certain days the sea and the sky would blend into each other.

He knew those days at sea when time was not even thought about. Everything was eternal. If you had to die, why couldn't you be at one with the sky and the sea, smelling the salt water and watching the pelicans make their awkward dives? Maybe if you had that memory stuck into your soul? Maybe then whatever was the force that prevailed would allow you the eternity you wanted.

He sipped the iced tea and thought about the gun. It would be quick and it would be over. His father had done it. Ernest would do it. Ernest did do it. He thought about Ernest and 1941. He wouldn't do it then. There would be reasons, car accidents, plane crashes, the near and the not so near escapes with bumps and scratches. If a man had to do it there must be good reason.

Reason, he thought. Reason was about to get everyone into a war in Ernest's letter just as reason had led to the Falklands War.

He read some more.

The phone call from Demarest woke me up. Could we meet for breakfast at a ham and egger near my hotel? He no longer had an office and didn't have a staff car at his disposal- and he said he damned well was not going to lower himself to ask for one.

I saw him in the back booth in the restaurant. He was wearing aviator glasses that reflected the room and all its comings and goings.

"I met with Kimmel," he said. "We talked right past each other. Kimmel's spit and polish in all the wrong places. Loves the Battleship Row display of forces, loves the airplanes wing-to-wing and doesn't really want to hear how we may be out-gunned and flying the 1935 version of a fighter plane. He's living in an Abbott and Costello service comedy, and he doesn't even know it."

I said that maybe we could get Kimmel a ticket to "Buck Privates," or better yet, "Wings."

"He wouldn't get the connection," Demarest said. "I spoke with Army command here, too. Some of them are worried, but not enough to rock the boat.

There may be a shark in their waters, but everyone is hoping that it'll bite someone else and go away."

"You're not going to stick around here?" I asked.

"No, by mutual agreement, I'm heading to where there's a real war. I'll be attached to the mission in London. Looks like we'll be holding up the Limeys, propping up their resistance to Hitler. Want to know what I think?"

I nodded.

"I think we're looking for an excuse to jump into the war. Maybe that's what we're doing with MacArthur in Manila, dangling an old man in front of a shark, or hell, maybe even here, although it's a longer way from Tokyo to get here. Say they attack Manila. Roosevelt would have his excuse."

I wished him good luck in London.

"I won't be surprised to see you over there when the war breaks out for us," he said.

"When the war breaks out?" I asked.

"Soon enough, " he said.

He shook my hand and left.

I got roped into another soiree at Aunt Grace's, this time with the promise of scintillating conversation, interesting people, fine wine and band music. I told her that Miss Marty still was in the Far East, but I could bring a substitute in the person of Floyd Martin, a young writer I knew.

We arrived in Martin's Jalopy, which was a bit of a contrast to the new Buicks, Cadillacs, and Lincolns parked around her house. A quartet consisting of a piano, saxophone, drums and bass played some of the popular tunes, "In the Mood," "Fools Rush in," and I'll Never Smile Again," among them.

The place was packed with civilians and military in dress uniform. Though the music was good, few were dancing. Cocktail party chitchat had the ball and didn't seem like it was going to yield to fun.

Martin nodded toward one of the Japanese servants who stood near a group of naval officers and their dates. I winked back at Martin, and we moved in close to the group.

"The death ray, of course," Martin said.

"Gordon relies on it extensively," I said.

One of the naval officers turned toward our conversation and joined in.

"He may use it against Ming," he said. "I can't wait to see what happens next."

"Well don't forget about how powerful those rocket engines are," I said.

We had the attention of the Japanese servant. His ear was cocked toward us.

"Commander Gordon is one of the best," Martin said.

"We could use someone like that in our outfit," the naval officer said, laughing.

"I wouldn't be surprised if he showed up over here with that death ray," I said. "Ming better watch it."

Martin and I walked off toward the bar after talking about Flash Gordon. When we looked back, we noticed the servant with the tray was gone.

"You think he's on the short wave wireless telling Tokyo about Flash Gordon?" Martin laughed.

"Bluffing might be our best weapon," I said. "Someone yells 'Shark in the water!' do you go swimming?"

"Only if you're a fish," Martin said. "Then you have no choice."

The image of Clapp's 13 foot-long marlin came to mind, hanging on that icehouse hook.

It didn't matter how big you might get. In the end, there wouldn't be much left, only guesses of where your scars had been and how much power you really had.

Everyone would tell a different tale.

Ernest

He remembered receiving the letter in New York. It came with a Honolulu postmark. He had put it in a drawer without reading it at first. There had been no need. Ernest had beaten the letter to New York and was in a good mood, happy to be back in the States, he said. The drinks would flow at Ernest's hotel, and all sorts of people would visit, writers, musicians, boxers and newspaper columnists.

Ernest would head south toward Washington with Miss Marty to tell his friend at Treasury what he thought about Chiang and China and Kimmel and Pearl Harbor. Ahead lay Havana and Pilar, the Gulfstream and yes, the War.

The War would come and change everything. America would get very sober and then very drunk on what America would become, a replacement for the French and the British Empires.

The letter got moved, along with a bunch of papers and books, to Bogota and eventually to Miami. After the shotgun had taken its toll, he looked for his brother in memories, in photos and old newspaper articles.

The book he wrote about his brother was already a best seller. Finding the letter and finally opening it was a comfort, a message from the Ernest who was at the top of his life, before the headaches and the depression and the anger would bring him down.

What Santiago had said that day on Mauna Kea _" some shotgun for birds. You gotta get close with a shotgun. The lion would have to eat the barrels while you pulled the triggers." It had to have stuck - the thought of the gun and a lion. Ernest had hunted lions and watched them die a quick death.

Was it Ernest's way of honoring Santiago by putting him in a small boat in the Gulfstream, fighting Clapp's Marlin all the way to a Nobel Prize?

He remembered the pain in his legs. They could hurt for another day. He would take the pills, but in the end he knew where he had hidden his gun.

He laughed as he thought of the revolver and how he had loaded all six chambers. Force of habit, he thought.

You wouldn't get a second pull on the trigger.

He was tired.

He would try to nap.

Later there would be some dinner and talk about what the doctors might attempt and how he might get healthy, perhaps without his legs and he would melt some more inside as they looked at him and tried to imagine the man he once was.

He knew that puzzled look of those who hadn't seen him in several months.

"Where was Les?" the look said.

This was all there was.

He looked up at the portrait of Ernest in the fisherman's sweater. There was dignity. There was resolve. Perhaps there was peace.

Tomorrow he would read the letter again and take more pills.

Ernest was right.

It didn't matter how big you might get.

In the end, there wouldn't be much left, only guesses of where your scars had been and how much power you really had.

Everyone would tell a different tale.

#

WHERE PLANE FOUND: X marks the spot where rescuers found the wrecked army bomber and its crew in the Kohala mountains Thursday. Dotted line represents new trail rescuers had to cut.

A newspaper map describing where the B-18 had crashed on the Big Island.

Epilogue

I was in Fort Myers on September 13, 1982, getting ready to go on air at WCAI, a progressive country radio station that featured the Eagles; Crosby, Stills and Nash, Willie Nelson and Dolly Parton.

The two-thirty ABC News feed brought the news that Leicester Hemingway had killed himself. The news hit me hard, but it wasn't a surprise. I had watched my friend go from a robust raconteur to a withered old man. We had been friends for five years, had worked together on publications and had laughed our way with vigor at the foibles of the powerful and the famous.

Along with his brother Ernest, we shared a birth city, Oak Park, Illinois. Ernest once described the town as a place of broad lawns and narrow minds. It was a place where people went to behave. Safe to say, it didn't measure up for the Hemingway brothers, and it didn't measure up for me. Respectability tends to destroy creativity. The western suburbs of Chicago were dens of respectability where if you did all the right things, you would get to be the boss in an enterprise that would stand out just so far. Not flashy, not trashy, but a good job, an honorable profession would be your reward. Everyone you met was white, or they were some servant or deliveryman who didn't hang around after dark.

If you were creative, you left. If you were too young to leave, you found a way to escape. For me, part of the escape plan was reading Ernest Hemingway. There was an assertion of freedom in his stories. No one ran away from adventure to meet with his staff at the Rexall drug store. You were at war; you were hunting, you were drunk, out on the Gulfstream, in an African Safari. No one was getting their brown wingtips shined while he read the Wall Street Journal.

I was in Elmhurst July 2, 1961.

Elmhurst was an Oak Park knock-off. My friends and I referred to the place as "a town too dead to die." Ernest's death hit hard that day. I was a teenage kid who knew very little about how Ernest had fallen apart in his final years. The image was robust. Courage was grace under pressure, and a man stood up to adventure. Later I would learn that platitudes and guns were only one side of the coin. If you believed only in the image, you were doing yourself a disservice. Being human was complicated, especially for Ernest Hemingway and later, I would learn, for his brother Leicester. People would meet him and say, "You look just like Hemingway!" "I am Hemingway," he'd reply. "No," one woman asserted. "I mean Hemingway Hemingway!"

Imagine telling someone your name and being accused of lying.

I made a mistake studying English at a private college in Southern Illinois. It was to be a pathway to becoming a writer. It was cruel and unusual punishment, an affliction of affectation by miserably dried up people who would rather be mildly clever than honestly entertaining and informing. The instructors all had their area of expertise that almost no other person on the planet cared about. That, of course, was their ticket to their doctorate. Find someone or something hanging around the periphery of someone big and research this marginality until the powers-that-be caved in and handed you your doctorate. These were the guardians of the language, the sticks in the mud who couldn't get past Tennyson and wouldn't let anyone else get past him either.

Beat poetry?

Noir literature?

Black voices?

Decidedly not.

There would always be a supercilious laugh directed toward anyone who hadn't honored *Piers Plowman*, a Middle English allegorical narrative poem, before bringing up someone like Nelson Algren, best known for writing *The Man with the Golden Arm,* a 1949 novel that won the National Book Award.

I often wondered how many of my professors had chased creative people into fields other than writing -- painting, film, broadcasting, music- where no one had to worry about the tyranny of a misspelled word or out of place comma.

Later, my radio career would introduce me to other rebels. Sometimes we'd deliberately misspell news copy at stations where I worked. It was an inside joke to read, "Prezident raygun is cumming 2 myammee 2 morro 2 meat width sivick litres. Hill bee in myamee threw 2s day."

It sounded good. It was good. It was a nod to the oral tradition before everyone had an alphabet, when rhyming helped people remember stories or nautical directions like the Hawaiians had done.

Story was king. That's what you learned from the writings of Ernest and Leicester. A press release or a news item could turn into a sailing adventure to Bimini or a safari in Africa. Story was all around you. You just had to plug in.

I never got through *Piers Plowman*. I know it's considered a classic and is probably worth reading. It's a look back some seven hundred years to what some of us once were.

I did meet Nelson Algren. It was 1971. He was going out with the mother of one of my friends. I was invited over for a small get together.

On the way over, I thought about what another friend, Danny Michaels had told me about Algren. Danny had been a writer on one of the hip Chicago entertainment magazines in the mid-fifties. During the world premiere of the Otto Preminger produced film, "The Man With the Golden Arm," Danny was assigned to write about Algren.

I had asked Danny what that was like.

"We stopped and had a lot of drinks," he said. "He kept buying and kept saying he was being screwed by Preminger. Algren was supposed to write the screenplay for his book, but Preminger said no to that. He even changed the ending."

I used the Chicago custom of parking illegally in an alley and entered the party through the kitchen. There was a guy with his head stuck in the open refrigerator. I said hello.

He turned around and said, "Hey, I'm Nelson Algren. Do you know where Yolanda keeps the mustard?"

We stood there talking "Chicago-ese." The mayor was a crook, and the cops were on the take, the White Sox were the workingman's team, the Cubs weren't worth a comment, and somehow everything that was wrong with the city made you love it even more.

After we had a few beers and some large sandwiches, our hostess came in and made us come to her living room to where the rest of the guests gathered.

I never got to ask Algren about being taken by Otto Preminger.

Years later, I did ask Les Hemingway about Algren.

"Good writer, one of the best," he said. "Ernest wrote a letter to Scribners in the early forties saying Algren was a talent they should look at."

Scribners didn't listen to Ernest. Algren's biggest book, *The Man With the Golden Arm* went to Doubleday.

Scribners didn't listen to Leicester, either. His biggest book, *My Brother, Ernest Hemingway* went to World Publishing.

At least it didn't go to Otto Preminger.

Harry Wishard with the Ernest Hemingway photo.

Ray Pace is the author of _Bearstone Blackie, Detective_, a collection of stories about a bear who investigates fairy tales. The work has been described as sardonic wit and political satire.

Among his books are: _Captain Mike's Honolulu Fright Night Tour_ and _Hemingway, Memories of Les_, a memoir of his friendship with Leicester Hemingway, N.Y. Times best-selling author of _My Brother, Ernest Hemingway._

Pace is President of Hawaii Writers Guild. He lives in Waikoloa Village on the Big Island of Hawaii. He can be reached at raypacewrites@gmail.com or visit his website www.raypaceatlarge.com

Follow the Hawaii Writers Guild on www.hawaiiwritersguild.com or on Facebook at Hawaii Writers Guild.

Made in the USA
Columbia, SC
05 June 2017